Little Fish, Lost

by NANCY VAN LAAN

illustrated by JANE CONTEH-MORGAN

AN ANNE SCHWARTZ BOOK

atheneum
books for young readers

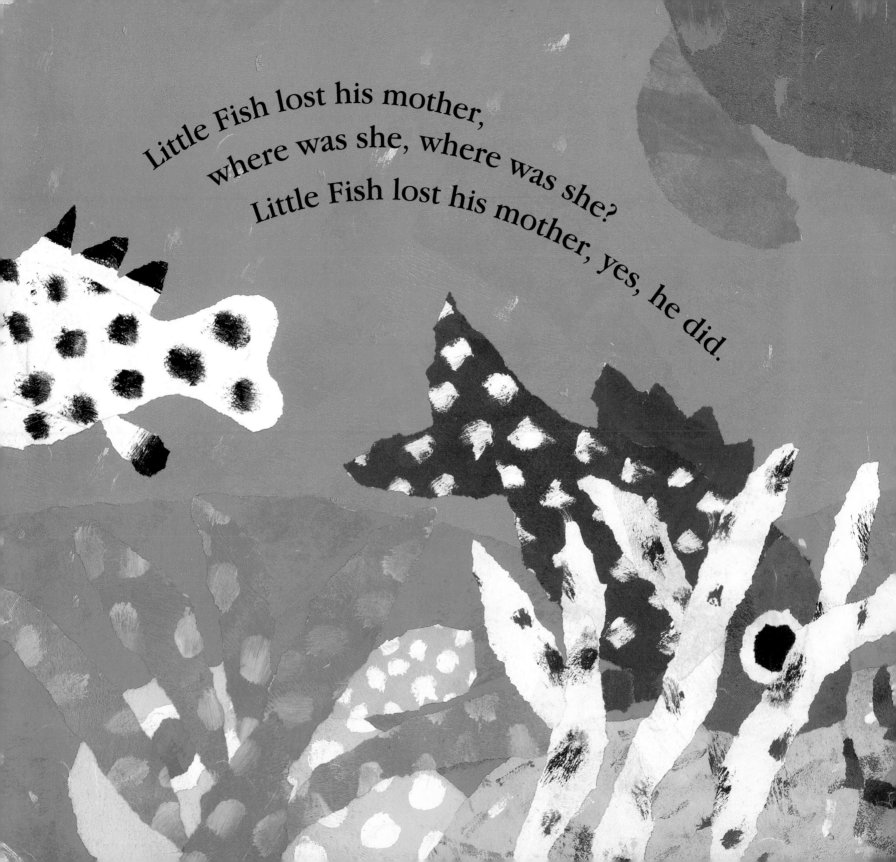

Little Fish lost his mother,
where was she, where was she?
Little Fish lost his mother, yes, he did.

Look look here. Look look there. Little Fish looked everywhere, but his mother, no, no, no, was not there.

As he swam all around,
up, up, up, down, down, down,
many fish, Little Fish saw.

Striped fish,

freckled fish,

whiskered fish,

puffy fish,

but his mother, no, no no, was not there.

To the top he swam, looking 'round,
where he saw other mothers, yes, he did.

Okapi, sipping water, sluppa-sup, with its young,

Hippo bathing baby, splish-a-splash, having fun,

Cheetah sprawling, scrub-a-scrub, cleaned its cub,

but *his* mother no, no, no, was not there.

Little Fish missed his mother,
where was she, where was she?
Little Fish missed his mother, yes, he did.

In the shallows, step-a-step,
was Jocana with her chick.

And in reeds with stalks, very thick,
was Spoonbill, each leg like a stick.

Little Fish whished away, tail a-flick!

Little Fish wanted his mother,
where was she, where was she?
Little Fish wanted his mother, yes, he did.

At the edge of the pond, tippa-taw, prowled Genet.
When she drank, lippa lap,
Little Fish's tail went SLAP!

CLAP! went Crawfish
on the bottom, snappa-snap.

Beetle scooped a tunnel, digga dig.

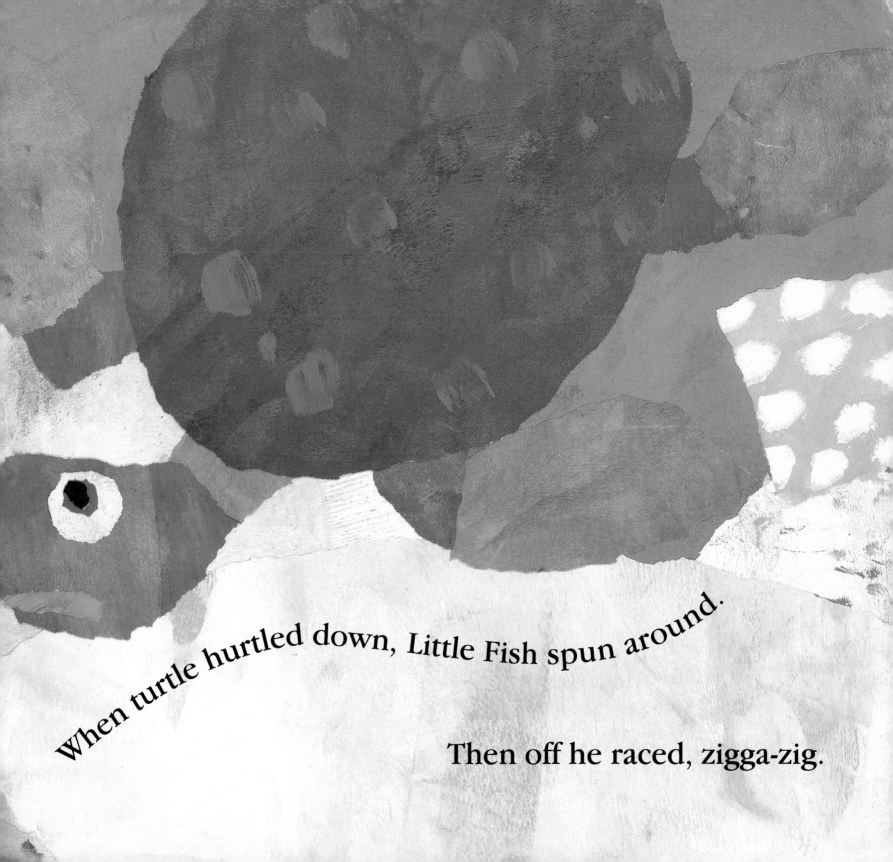

When turtle hurtled down, Little Fish spun around.

Then off he raced, zigga-zig.

Little Fish needed his mother,
where was she, where was she?
Little Fish needed his mother, yes, he did.

So Little Fish strayed way a-way to the deep, dark middle,
where a fish as big as it could be,
whipped its tail, woosh woosh,
stretched its mouth, gullumph gullumph,

and swallowed all the fishes it could see!

Oh, *where* was his mother,
where was she, where was she?
Little Fish cried for his mother, yes, he did.

Then all alone,
he slipped between two stones,
tail and fin tucked in, thinny thin.

It was there, right there, Little Fish found his mother,
who wondered where, where, where had *he* been!

Was he happy,
was he?

Was she happy,
was she?

Through reeds, hidden deep,
side by side, swim swim leap.

Little Fish found his mother,

yes,
he did!

For my good friend Jane, who always knows where I am
—N. V. L.

For my four little fish: Bundu, Obai, Sorie, Amie
—J. C-M.

Atheneum Books for Young Readers
An imprint of Simon & Schuster Children's Publishing Division
1230 Avenue of the Americas
New York, New York 10020

Book design by Ann Bobco
The text of this book is set in Garamond ITC.
The illustrations are rendered in collage.

First Edition
Printed in Hong Kong by South China Printing Co. (1988) Ltd.
10 9 8 7 6 5 4 3 2 1

Library of Congress Cataloging-in-Publication Data
Van Laan, Nancy.
Little Fish, lost / by Nancy Van Laan ;
illustrated by Jane Conteh-Morgan.—1st ed.
p.   cm.
"An Anne Schwartz book."
Summary: Little Fish loses his mother in an African pond and searches
everywhere for her, seeing all kinds of animals in the process.
ISBN 0-689-81331-7
[1. Fishes—Fiction. 2. Animals—Fiction. 3. Zoology—Africa—Fiction.
4. Africa—Fiction. 5. Mother and child—Fiction. 6. Stories in rhyme.]
I. Conteh-Morgan, Jane, ill. II. Title.
PZ8.3.V47L1   1998
[E]—dc20
96-26344